MW01132144

Horsenapped!

STORM CLIFF
STABLES

by Lisa Mullarkey
Illustrated by Paula Franco

Calico

An Imprint of Magic Wagon
www.abdopublishing.com

www.abdopublishing.com

Published by Magic Wagon, a division of ABDO, PO Box 398166, Minneapolis, Minnesota 55439. Copyright © 2015 by Abdo Consulting Group, Inc. International copyrights reserved in all countries. No part of this book may be reproduced in any form without written permission from the publisher. Calico™ is a trademark and logo of Magic Wagon.

Printed in the United States of America, North Mankato, Minnesota.
052014
092014

Written by Lisa Mullarkey
Illustrations by Paula Franco
Edited by Tamara L. Britton and Megan M. Gunderson
Cover and interior design by Candice Keimig

Library of Congress Cataloging-in-Publication Data

Mullarkey, Lisa, author.
  Horsenapped! / by Lisa Mullarkey ; illustrated by Paula Franco.
    pages cm. -- (Storm Cliff Stables)
  Summary: Bree has decided to give up riding after a bad fall at home, but she still enjoys summers at Storm Cliff Stables with her close friends, and learning how to care for the horses and other animals--but when the animals start disappearing one by one Bree is determined to solve the mystery.
  ISBN 978-1-62402-051-3
1. Riding schools--Juvenile fiction. 2. Horse stealing--Juvenile fiction. 3. Horsemanship--Juvenile fiction. 4. Best friends--Juvenile fiction. [1. Mystery and detective stories. 2. Horsemanship--Fiction. 3. Horse stealing--Fiction. 4. Best friends--Fiction. 5. Friendship--Fiction.] I. Title.
  PZ7.M91148Ho 2015
  813.6--dc23
                            2014005833

Table of Contents

Chapter 1
Full-Time Barn Rat

"Got a minute, Bree?" asked Aunt Jane as she poked her head into our cabin.

Aunt Jane isn't my real aunt. She's the owner of Storm Cliff Stables. Everyone at camp calls her Aunt Jane. Storm Cliff Stables is where I met my best friends: Avery, Esha, and Jaelyn. We call ourselves the Core Four.

"Sure," I said. "What's up?"

Jaelyn pulled her riding boots on. "Is this private? Do you want us to leave?"

Aunt Jane smiled. "Nope. Not private at all. I just wanted to see how you're doing, Bree. Do you miss riding? Are you bored at all?"

"Bored?" I asked. "How can I be bored with all of the animals at Storm Cliff Stables? And it's not just the horses. There's Freckles, Golden Girl, Gaston . . . the farm animals are majorly cute!" I pointed to the schedule on the desk. "There are so many activities planned, there's no time to be bored." I held up my bathing suit. "And I swim every day."

"And we do all sorts of arts and crafts projects together," said Jaelyn.

She held up the plaster hoofprints I had made from Pip and Squeak, the newest miniature horses at Storm Cliff Stables.

Avery pulled her hair into a ponytail. "And the campfires, archery lessons, nature walks. Bree does everything but ride."

Aunt Jane ran her hand through her hair. "Okay. You've proven that you're quite the busy camper, Bree. As long as you're happy with your decision to become a full-time barn rat." She gave my arm a squeeze. "If you wanted to ride again, we could . . ."

I thought back to the day in winter when I was thrown from my horse. I shuddered. "No way, Aunt Jane. I'll never ride again." I rubbed my collarbone. "I broke this bone and dislocated my shoulder. It was awful." I pointed to Avery's helmet. "If I hadn't been wearing one of those, I wouldn't be here today. At least that's what my parents said."

Aunt Jane put her hand over her heart. "Oh, Bree! Thank goodness you were wearing your helmet. Safety first. Right Esha?"

Esha didn't always like to follow the rules. Sometimes she tried to ride without her helmet.

Esha blew on her nails. "Yep." She rolled her eyes. "A smart rider is a safe rider."

Aunt Jane had said that to us at least a million times. But I was never too sure if Esha believed it.

Esha waved her nails in front of me. "You know what they say, Bree. If you fall off a horse, you gotta get right back on."

"Not me," I said. "I'm done. I'd rather work with the horses and groom them."

Esha clicked her tongue. "Muckin' stalls is gross. I love brushin' Queenie, but groomin' a bunch of horses all day long is bor-ing!"

Queenie was the bay Morgan mare Esha rode at camp. Sometimes I'd groom her again after Esha finished so I could get her coat extra clean and shiny. But I never told Esha.

"Not boring to me," I said. "Besides," I continued, "Cupcake isn't here."

Cupcake was a tricolored leopard Appaloosa mare that I rode each year here at camp. She was moved to a new stable a few months ago.

"That made my decision even easier," I said. "If I want to be an equine veterinarian or even a regular vet, I need to learn everything I can. The sooner the better."

Jaelyn tightened the cap on Esha's nail polish so it wouldn't spill.

"All the horses love Bree, Aunt Jane," Jaelyn said. "She keeps them safe, too. If it weren't for Bree noticing that nail sticking out of the door to Blue's stall, he could have scraped his belly on it."

"Remember when Blue was spooked by a rabbit on the trail last year?" I asked.

Jaelyn nodded. "You were the only one who was able to calm him down."

Aunt Jane slowly nodded. "I remember. Maybe that's why I sometimes forget you're just 12 years old. Layla says she's impressed by your attention to detail. She says you're the best stall mucker around. Better than most of the paid workers."

Layla is one of the counselors and is in charge of our cabin.

I beamed.

"And Dr. Samuels said you're a great helper and you ask such thoughtful questions. He thinks you'll make a finer vet than he is one day," said Aunt Jane.

Avery patted me on the back. "Thanks to Bree, Sapphire's stall is squeaky clean. Sapphire loves her as much as she loves me."

"Almost as much," I said.

Sapphire was a chestnut Thoroughbred mare. Avery jumped her every day.

Esha smirked. "Sapphire doesn't like me much though."

It was true. Sapphire did seem to get cranky whenever Esha showed up in her stall. She would swish her tail and flatten her ears.

"Maybe because I'm so flashy," said Esha.

"Or bossy," Jaelyn said.

Aunt Jane laughed.

But Esha didn't get mad. She never got mad. "Yep. I'm bossy," she said. "And proud of it!"

"Okay, Bree," said Aunt Jane. "Now that I know you're as happy as Freckles the pig in a puddle of mud, I was wondering if you'd do me a favor."

I'd do anything for Aunt Jane. "Sure! What kind of favor?"

Aunt Jane crossed her fingers. "Would you be willing to spend 30 minutes each day with the Pony Girls?"

The Pony Girls are the new eight-year-old campers. Esha thought they were annoying, but we had all been Pony Girls our first year at camp.

"You could teach them about life as a barn rat. They have stable management classes a few times a week, but this is an optional activity for the girls who love *all* the animals at Storm Cliff Stables. Not just the horses."

"Like me!" I said as I jumped up and down. "I would love to! I was eight years old when I became a barn rat." I wrapped my arms around Aunt Jane's waist.

"Congratulations," said Jaelyn. "That's really cool. I'll make you a sign for the class. We can hang it outside the stable."

"Hang it on the barn," said Aunt Jane. "That way, the girls can see the miniature horses and learn to take care of the other animals, too. Can you start tomorrow? You can introduce Pip and Squeak first. None of the Pony Girls have seen the miniature horses before. After that you can teach them about Freckles, Golden Girl, and the rest of the animals."

I nodded. "Thanks, Aunt Jane. I won't let you down." Then I laughed. "I'll explain how Golden Girl isn't a *typical* chicken. A *crazy* chicken? Yep!"

"Sounds good, Bree. I knew you were the right one for the job. You'll be a great role model to all of the Pony Girls. They'll learn a lot from you." Then she leaned in close to my face. "Now don't ever give me a reason to fire you, okay?" She winked.

Now I crossed my fingers. "Oh, I won't! Promise!"

After a round of high fives, she left.

"I know Freckles is a pig. Who's Golden Girl?" asked Jaelyn.

"Golden Girl is a crazy chicken who likes to sit on Freckles. And on Gaston, the goat. Sometimes she sits on Pip or Squeak, too. It's really funny."

"Don't the animals get mad?" asked Esha. "I'd be steamin' if a chicken sat on me."

"They don't even notice," I said. "And Golden Girl lays *massive* eggs. Dr. Samuels thinks her eggs could get her into the *Guinness Book of World Records*." I glanced at my watch. "Want to go meet Golden Girl before you go riding?"

And just like that, we headed down to the barn. I waved to the farmhands as we passed them.

"Who are they?" asked Avery.

"Aunt Jane's workers," I said. "She calls them her farm family. I help them take care of the animals. They mostly look out for the pigs and cows. And they make sure the veggies are growing over there." I pointed to a huge patch of land behind the barn. "Sometimes they're so busy, I don't think they even notice me. But if I don't see them here, I'm not allowed to work with the animals. Aunt Jane is pretty strict about that."

Avery scanned the area. "There are the goats and sheep." She pointed to one of the other pens. "There's Freckles."

"Pip and Squeak are over there grazing," I said pointing to the large fenced-in area. "But I don't see Golden Girl anywhere."

"Come out, come out, wherever you are," sang Jaelyn.

"She's probably inside the barn on top of the haystack. Or she could be sitting under Daisy. She never leaves that poor cow alone!"

We walked inside the barn and looked around.

Nothing.

"Daisy, where did Golden Girl get to?"

Daisy looked straight ahead and ignored me.

"Is she scared of us?" asked Avery.

"Look at her tail," I said. "If she's afraid, her tail will be tucked between her legs."

"It's hangin' straight down," said Jaelyn. "What does that mean?"

"That she's happy," I said as I rubbed her side. "Don't feel like talking much today, do you, Daisy?" Then I turned to the girls. "If Golden Girl isn't in here or out there, where is she?"

"Lost?" asked Jaelyn.

"Lost?" repeated Esha. Her eyes grew as big as the milking stools. "You *lost* a chicken? Already?" She smacked her lips. "Aunt Jane is gonna fire you!"

Fire me? My face felt like it was on fire. *Some role model I am.*

"Great," I said. "Just great. My first day on the job and I'm about to get fired for losing a crazy chicken."

I tried to smile.

But I couldn't.

I wanted to fly the coop.

After Jaelyn, Avery, and Esha left, I brushed Freckles down and checked his tail and hooves. I wasn't sure why I bothered because I knew he'd plop right down in the mud as soon as I left!

After I put some fresh water in his trough, I opened up the plastic container of treats. His "treats" were leftovers from the kitchen. I shook the container. "Looks like you have hash browns, hard bagels, and waffles today." I added some of this to the grain in the food trough. "Fit for a king."

When I left the pen, I saw Dr. Samuels standing by Pip in the pasture. "Dr. Samuels! I didn't know you were coming today."

I walked over to the fence and leaned on it. I lowered my voice so I wouldn't spook Pip or

Squeak. "I have great news. Starting tomorrow, I'm going to teach the Pony Girls all about being a barn rat. Won't they just love Pip and Squeak?"

Dr. Samuels smiled. "That's great news. The little ones are always eager to learn." He ran his fingers through Pip's forelock. "I've got some bad news, though. I was actually here checking up on Pip and Squeak an hour ago. Look what I found." He held up a nail. "I just showed Layla." He put it in his bag. "Aunt Jane isn't going to be happy about it. This is the second time in the last two weeks that I've had to take a nail out of Pip's hoof." He scanned the ground. "Where are they coming from?"

I had no idea.

"Pip and Squeak are out here grazing most of the day. I haven't seen any nails around here," I said. I thought about the barn. "I clean their stalls out every day. Sometimes twice. I'm really careful. Honest."

Dr. Samuels patted my back. "Don't fret, Bree. I'm sure you are. That's why someone checks all of Aunt Jane's horses from head to hoof daily. Keeps them healthy. They'd be in real trouble if we didn't and something like this went unnoticed."

I offered Pip a sugar cube. To thank me, he rubbed his head against my cheek.

Dr. Samuels looked over my shoulder and waved. "Bree, this here is my son, Brent."

I didn't even know Dr. Samuels had a son!

I turned around to see a tall kid wearing a long-sleeved shirt and jeans and holding a hammer. He waved. "Hi. Do you work for Aunt Jane?"

"Yep," I said. "Well, sort of. I'm a camper but I'm not riding this year. I'm helping out in the barn and stables instead."

Brent looked confused. "You came to a horse camp but you don't ride?" He wiped away a drop of sweat from his nose. "That's weird."

"Not weird at all," I said. *Not as weird as you wearing a long-sleeved shirt in 95-degree weather*, I thought. "I used to ride but I got hurt." I wanted to change the subject. "Do you ride?"

"Nah," he said. "I work here. Aunt Jane has me fix fences, paint some of the buildings.

Stuff like that. I'm saving the money I make for college next year."

"Aren't you hot?" I asked.

"I don't want to get a bad sunburn," he said. "Been there, done that. It wasn't fun."

Dr. Samuels pursed his lips. "You aren't dropping nails around here are you, Brent? Aunt Jane pays you to fix fences and solve problems. Not cause them."

Brent looked annoyed. "Not me. If I take ten nails, I use ten nails."

Dr. Samuels unlatched the gate and walked toward Freckles. "This here pig is an escape artist. He's a quick one, Bree. He breaks free of his pen at least once a week."

We followed Dr. Samuels into the pen. Freckles was busy rolling around in a mixture of mud and hay.

I groaned. "I just cleaned him."

"Guess he's making some homemade

sunscreen," said Dr. Samuels. "The mud and hay will protect him from the sun."

"Hey, that's sort of why you're wearing those clothes," I said.

Brent ignored me. "He's a cute little thing, isn't he?"

Freckles snorted.

"Did you know he starred in his own commercial last year?" I said.

Brent looked surprised. "Really? How cool is that!"

"Aunt Jane said he's a celebrity around here," I said.

"Maybe I'll do a story on him," said Brent. "I could find the commercial and insert it into the story." He pretended to tip a hat to me. "Thanks for the idea."

"What do you mean?" I asked.

Dr. Samuels sighed. "Brent is chasing fancy dreams. I tell him a vet's life is a good life, but he wants to go to school to make movies. Be a movie star."

"Wow," I said. "Really?"

Brent threw up his hands. "Not a movie star, Dad." He rolled his eyes. "I want to be a newscaster. Report stories. Interview people." He dug his feet into the grass. "I'm good at it."

"Nonsense stuff," said Dr. Samuels. "You should be doing what Bree's doing every day. Taking care of animals. It's rewarding. Makes you feel good inside. Instead you're on that computer of yours all day long wasting time."

Brent shook his head. "I'm not wasting time. I'm putting my clips together for my college application. Every time I upload a video, I get at least a thousand hits." He shoved his hands into his pockets. "I was hoping to interview Anna Wainwright this summer. I could have gotten a million hits!"

Anna was Aunt Jane's niece who had won two Olympic gold medals for jumping. She was supposed to come to camp this summer but had to change her plans.

"I was so bummed she canceled," said Brent.

"We were too," I said. "My friend Avery loves Anna Wainwright. She plans on making the US Equestrian Team one day just like Anna. Did you know that Anna used to ride Sapphire, who is right down there in that stable? Avery rides her now."

"Really?" said Brent. "Are you sure Anna actually rode her?"

"More than that," I said. "That's the horse she learned to jump with."

Brent smiled. "Thanks for telling me. Now I'm double bummed Anna isn't coming this summer. Interviewing Anna could have impressed some of the colleges I'm applying to. Right, Dad?"

Dr. Samuels focused on Freckles. "If you

want to impress me, Brent," he said as he pointed to a small opening in the fence by the woods, "board that up, will you? Don't want anyone wandering through and getting a bad case of the ivy."

"The ivy?" I asked.

"Poison ivy," said Brent. "That trail is crawling with it."

"Oddest thing," said Dr. Samuels. "That trail leads to our house about a mile away. I could walk it and be here in ten minutes. But it's so full of the stuff that I'd be laid up for weeks if I even stepped foot in there. I haven't seen another speck of poison ivy round this camp or on my property. Just that trail."

I started to walk toward the trail to get a peek but Brent stopped me. "Don't even go over there. Trust me. You'll be itching before lunch."

Dr. Samuels shook his head and pointed to Brent. "Get to work. Aunt Jane pays you good money. Earn it." He looked at his watch. "Bree and I have some work of our own to do."

That reminded me of Golden Girl.

"Have either of you seen Golden Girl?" I asked. "I can't find her anywhere. I haven't seen her since last night."

Dr. Samuels glanced around the farm. "Did you check on top of the haystack?"

"I checked on top of *everything*," I said.

"She'll be back soon," said Brent. "I mean, you'll find her soon." He held up his hammer. "That's why I'm here. Freckles isn't the only animal who likes to escape. There's so much land around here, sometimes the animals like to check it out."

"He's probably right, Bree," said Dr. Samuels. "Golden Girl will show up. Could have wandered down to the stable. You never know." He ran his finger down the clipboard. "How about you tell the Pony Girls about Pip and Squeak's teeth? Thanks to you, I'm going to be filing Pip's tomorrow. Tell them exactly what you told me a few days ago. Then I'll let each girl look inside Pip's mouth. They'll be able to see the points before I file them down. What do you think?"

"That sounds like an amazing idea! Hear that Pip? Tomorrow you're going to get your teeth fixed." I gave Pip and Squeak each a piece of apple from my pocket, and if I didn't know any better, I could have sworn I saw them both smile.

"Do you like it?" asked Jaelyn. "It's dry now."

She waved a poster that said "Welcome Pony Girls! You Are Now Barn Rats." Pictures of the barn animals were on it too.

"I would have drawn Golden Girl but I don't know what she looks like," said Jaelyn.

I held up the poster to get a better look. "It looks great," I said.

Jaelyn was an incredible artist. She loved bringing her sketchbook on trail rides with Blue.

Esha glanced over. "You should put a *B* in front of the *R*. It should say 'Barn *Brats*.' The Pony Girls are whiny. I saw one cry last night because her s'more fell into the fire."

I shrugged.

"I don't think Aunt Jane would like Barn *Brats,* but it is pretty funny," said Avery.

"The eight-year-olds are cute," I said. "Not as cute as the baby farm animals though."

Avery looked out the window. "The campfire's starting in a few minutes. We'd better get going. I want a front-row seat."

Esha grabbed the poster. "I have an idea. Why don't we go to the barn and hang this up now?"

"Now?" said Avery. "It's dark outside."

"You're not afraid of the dark, are you?" asked Esha.

Avery didn't say anything.

"I'm not afraid of the dark," I said. "But we can't go. It's closed up for the night."

Esha folded her arms across her chest. "Do they have a lock on the barn door?"

I smiled and shook my head again. "Nope."

"A sign that says, 'The Core Four are not allowed to come to the barn when it's dark'?" asked Esha.

Avery sighed. "We aren't allowed near the animals unless an adult is there. Right, Bree?"

Before I could answer, Esha butted back in. "Actually, we aren't allowed to *work* with the animals unless an adult is there. We don't need one there if we're just lookin' at them. Do we, Bree?"

Avery grabbed a flashlight and suddenly looked a whole lot braver. "I guess it can't hurt as long as we bring our flashlights along. We'll only be there for a few minutes, right?"

I chewed on my lip. "Well ... I guess we weren't ever told we couldn't go. And if it's to get ready for my class tomorrow ..."

Jaelyn's face lit up. "While we're there, we can look for Golden Girl! Maybe she's back."

"Okay," I said. "I'm in. I know I'll feel better if I see Golden Girl tucked in safe and sound." I grabbed my flashlight. "But we can't stay too long and we have to go right to the campfire after." I leaned in close and whispered, "We can't let anyone know we were there. Got it?"

"Got it," said Esha.

Avery nodded.

"Maybe we shouldn't use our flashlights," said Jaelyn. "If someone sees the light, they could come to see who's sneaking around."

Avery turned white.

I grabbed her hand. "Stay with me, Avery. I know my way around there. No problem!"

But when we got to the barn, there was a problem. It was dark. Very dark. Couldn't-see-my-hand-in-front-of-my-face kind of dark.

"I can't see anything," said Avery. "I'm scared."

I squeezed her hand. She squeezed back.

We heard the faint hooting of an owl above the chatter of tree frogs and crickets. We could hear some shuffling in Freckles's pen and the scurrying of mice along the walls. They were probably looking for food.

I walked toward the side of the barn. There was a long bench that butted up against the side. "Let's hang the poster over here. We can move this bench tomorrow for the Pony Girls to sit on." I turned on my flashlight to prove the bench was there. Then I clicked it off. "Give me the tape."

Avery handed me a few pieces of tape while Jaelyn and Esha held the poster up on the wooden planks. "I hope it's not crooked," I said as I taped down the last corner.

"Let's go to the campfire," whispered Avery. "It's way too dark out here. Kinda creepy."

"In a minute, Avery," I said. "I want to see if Golden Girl is inside the barn." I slowly opened the door and ducked inside. The rest of the Core Four followed me. Once inside, we were relieved to see a dim light on in the corner of the barn by Daisy.

"Maybe she's afraid of the dark," said Esha.

I walked over to her. "Hiya, girl. Have you seen Golden Girl? I just want to make sure she's tucked in safe and warm."

Daisy batted her eyelashes and then went back to chewing some hay. Before I had a chance to look around, Esha started to yell.

"She's right here!" Esha pointed to the haystack in the corner of the barn. "There."

"Shhh!" I said. "You'll scare the animals."

I walked over to them. "Were you hiding *under* that hay today, Golden Girl?" I asked.

Golden Girl clucked and settled deeper into the hay.

"Now that we hung up the poster *and* found Golden Girl, can we please get out of here?" said Avery.

As I turned around to go, I saw a light flash outside the window. "Duck!" I said as I fell to the ground.

Everyone dropped to the floor.

"What are we ducking for?" asked Jaelyn.

"I saw a light," I whispered. I crawled along the floor and sat up with my back against the wall directly under the window.

"I didn't see anything," said Esha.

Jaelyn shook her head. "Me either."

Avery looked worried. "Was it a flashlight? Was it *right* outside the window?"

I put my finger to my mouth and whispered, "I hear something."

Some of the pigs were raising a ruckus.

We sat there for at least two minutes before anyone moved or spoke again.

Finally, Esha spoke. "What are they squawkin' about? Are the animals always so noisy at night?"

I shrugged. "I've never been here at night."

Avery crept over to me. "I knew we shouldn't have come." She closed her eyes and clasped her hands together. It looked like she was praying.

"No one will find out," I said. I inched up the wall and was able to peek through the corner of the glass.

"What do you see?" asked Esha.

"Nothing. It's so dark outside I can't see a thing."

But a minute later, I noticed something. "Wait, there's a faint light." I motioned for Avery, Esha, and Jaelyn to take a look. "Is that a flashlight over there?"

"Where?" asked Jaelyn.

"Over there. To the left." It was the exact place that Brent was putting up a fence earlier to block the poison ivy path. "I think I saw a moving light."

"A UFO for sure," said Esha. She raised her eyebrows at Avery and smiled.

"Good try, Esha. Sorry to break it to you, but I'm not scared of UFOs at all."

Esha snapped her fingers. "Darn!" She peered out the window again. "I see a light, too. Look, there it is again. And again, and again," she said. Then she turned around and threw her hands up in the air. "Fireflies. We're scared of a bunch of fireflies."

"Fireflies?" asked Avery. "You think so?"

"I know so," said Esha.

I wasn't too sure, but I didn't want to spook Avery any more than she was already.

"Whatever it is, it's far away now," I said. "We need to get to the campfire before anyone notices we're not there."

We crawled to the barn door and then scurried into the dark.

Down the hill, we could see the glow from the campfire. The firelight was flickering through the bushes. You could see shadows moving but we were too far away to see who the campers were.

"Ready?" I asked.

We started to go down the hill when I thought of all the noise that the pigs had made. "Maybe we should check on the pigs. Especially Freckles. He's in the bigger pen all by himself."

Avery tugged on my arm. "Let's just go. Freckles is fine."

I flicked on my flashlight in the direction of the pen. "I just want to be sure."

The light seemed to catch the smaller pigs by surprise. They snorted and quickly scattered in every direction. When I moved the flashlight to the right, I expected to see Freckles in his mud bath.

But that's not what I saw.

I didn't see anything in the pen.

Nothing at all.

I quickly moved the flashlight back and forth. To the left, I could see that the opening in the fence by the poison ivy path wasn't boarded up.

I gasped.

"Freckles isn't fine," I said. "He's not fine at all. He's gone!"

"Well," said Avery as she put her plate on the table at breakfast the next day, "was Freckles in his pen this morning?"

I buttered my bagel. "Yep."

"So you were wrong," said Esha. "He wasn't missin'. Not much of an escape artist."

"I'm telling you, his pen was empty last night," I said. "But when I got there this morning, Layla was already feeding Freckles. And I got there super early to look for him."

"What about the opening in the fence?" asked Jaelyn.

"It was blocked off again," I said. "But I know it wasn't last night. I'm positive."

Esha chomped on some bacon. "Obviously,

you were wrong. It's not like the pig could pry boards off the fence himself, ya know." She took another bite. "He was probably hidin' in a corner."

I dropped my bagel. "Do you really have to eat that bacon? I mean, we're talking about Freckles. A *pig*. That could be his brother or sister."

As much as I loved my friends, I could never understand how they ate meat. I'm a vegetarian.

Jaelyn pushed the bacon off of her plate and scrunched her nose. "Well, if you put it that way."

"Do you think I forgot to close the gate to the pen last night? Aunt Jane gets really mad when doors are left open. I don't want her thinking I'm not responsible. She could fire me." I put my head on the table. "But I know I closed it."

I looked around. No one was listening to me. Avery had her head stuck in a *Horse & Rider* magazine. Jaelyn was sketching a horse on her napkin, and Esha was off showing the girls from Cabin 3 her neon nails.

I got up, threw away my trash, and headed down to the barn.

A few minutes later, Aunt Jane walked up the path with six Pony Girls. After they arranged themselves on the bench, I went inside to get Pip and Squeak. When I brought them out, I heard the girls let out happy squeals.

"They are cuties, aren't they?" I asked. "How many of you think these are ponies?"

Every hand flew into the air.

I shook my head. "They aren't. Pip and Squeak are miniature horses. We have three miniatures on this farm: Pip, Squeak, and their cousin, Popcorn."

"They're so cute," said a little redheaded girl. "Can I ride them?"

"Sorry," I said. "You're too old to ride them. Anyone over three years old is too heavy. If you mounted them, you could hurt their spines."

She crossed her arms and pouted her lips.

"But the good news is that you can walk Pip and Squeak around the arenas, talk to them, and even help groom them today."

The little redheaded girl put her hands on her hips and smiled. "Now?"

"Not until I tell you some information about miniature horses," I said. "Like did you know that a miniature horse will never be taller than thirty-six inches? Pip is only thirty-three inches. Squeak is even smaller. Just like our horses in the stable down there, miniature horses come in lots of different colors. They have so many different shapes on their coats. In fact, Aunt Jane thought that Popcorn's coat looked like pieces of popcorn, so . . ."

"I named him Popcorn," said Aunt Jane. "Everyone will meet him soon enough."

The girls giggled.

I gave Pip a peppermint. "Pip is a lot like a regular horse," I said. "He needs to eat and exercise. But sometimes miniature horses get too much food and not enough exercise. That's not healthy, is it?"

The six girls shook their heads from side to side.

"If they eat too much, they get fat," I said. "It's called obese. We don't want an obese horse. So one of my jobs is to walk with the miniatures and make sure they get to go out to the pasture to run around over there. They don't like to be cooped up inside all day long."

Aunt Jane pointed to the girls and gave me a thumbs-up. They were hanging on every word I said! This was fun.

"Did you know that horses chew from side to side?" I asked. "And their teeth keep growing. In fact, they never stop growing. Sometimes they grow too big. That's why Pip has a little problem today," I said. "Would you like to know what it is?"

The Pony Girls kept bobbing their heads up and down.

"Pip has a toothache. Until we take care of it, Pip will be a little cranky," I said. "Do you know what he does when he's cranky?"

"What?" asked the girl with red hair.

"He chews on wood," I said. I bent over to pick up a chewed plank of wood from his stable door. "We had to replace this piece of wood the other day because Pip ruined it. You can see some splinters sticking out of it." I walked in front of the Pony Girls so they could get a better look.

"Pip would get in a lot of trouble at my house," said the redheaded girl. "He's bad."

"No," I said. "Pip isn't bad at all. In fact, when I saw the wood like this, I knew Pip must not be feeling well. And I noticed three other things. Pip had bad breath." I waved my hand in front of my nose. "Stinky! He wasn't eating as much as he usually did either. And then when I had to muck out his stall, I saw something really gross."

"Poop!" shouted six little voices.

"Yep. But not healthy poop. Pip's poop had grain and hay in it. That's when I knew he was sick. So, I did what any good barn rat would do."

"She told me," said Aunt Jane. "Then I called Dr. Samuels here. You all know him from your stable management class."

He waved at them. All but the redheaded girl waved back. She was too busy braiding the hair of the girl next to her.

I smiled at Aunt Jane and kept on talking. "Miniature horses have a lot more problems with their teeth than regular horses do. That's because they have a smaller head but they have the same number of teeth as a regular-sized horse. And their teeth are the same size as a bigger horse's teeth."

"So they get all squished inside?" asked the redhead.

"A-plus for you," I said. "You're smart."

"Smarter than you," she said.

"I'm smart too," said another Pony Girl, showing her dimples. Then another one said she was smarter than everyone in the *whole wide world*. And then one Pony Girl called another one dumb because she dropped her s'more into the campfire. It was chaos!

"Whoa," I said, wanting to raise my voice but knowing I shouldn't. "If you argue in front of Pip and Squeak, I'll have to take them inside." I let Squeak lap a peppermint out of my hand. "Miniatures need to have people with calm, quiet voices around them at all times. No yelling or arguing. Got it?"

Five heads bobbed up and down again. The redheaded girl was still telling everyone how smart she was. Aunt Jane had to whisper something in her ear to quiet her down.

"Pip has been losing his baby teeth," said Dr. Samuels. "Just like most of you have been doing over the last few years. But one of Pip's baby teeth, we call them caps, got stuck on his permanent tooth. That caused a problem. Horses don't like when that happens. They try to get the cap off."

The redhead spoke up again. "By eating wood?"

The other girls laughed.

"Actually," said Dr. Samuels, "you're right. He chewed the wood in hopes of getting the cap off since it's bothering him. Pip didn't like the bump that it caused right here." He pointed to Pip's jaw. "So yesterday I removed the cap. And today, he's feeling a lot better."

"But Pip still has a tiny problem with his teeth," I said. "His teeth aren't working when he puts them together. Some are too big. And pointy. So today, Dr. Samuels is going to float some of Pip's teeth. It's sort of like filing your nails. It doesn't hurt them. In fact, horses like it because that means they can eat without their teeth hurting."

Dr. Samuels put his hat light on and looked into Pip's mouth. "You can see how pointy some of Pip's teeth are. Those points can hurt his tongue and cheeks when he eats. Bree knew that the hay and grain in his poop meant that Pip wasn't able to chew his food that well. So he just swallowed the food without chewing and grinding it up. That's dangerous. So today, I'm going to take this float and make Pip's teeth even."

He held up a file that was attached to a long handle.

He called up the girls one by one and let them wear his hat to look into Pip's mouth.

"Can I file his tooth?" asked the redhead.

When Dr. Samuels explained that he had to do it in the stable to make sure Pip was safe, she rolled her eyes. She reminded me of Esha.

After everyone looked into Pip's mouth, Aunt Jane and I took the girls to meet Popcorn.

"Bravo," said Aunt Jane as we walked into the barn. "The Pony Girls love you, Bree. Let me bring them down to the Pavilion and get them some water and a snack before they pass out from this heat."

When Aunt Jane left, I headed back into the barn to check on Pip and Dr. Samuels. That's when I noticed Brent fiddling with the fence near the path.

I was about to go over to him when I saw him take a quick look around. Then he took some apples and carrots out from under his shirt and chucked them into the poison ivy path.

Strange.

Very strange.

I've heard of an apple a day keeps the doctor away, but did Brent think it kept away the poison ivy, too?

"Last one to reach the raft is a rotten egg!" I yelled as I ran toward the lake.

Esha took off running and was the first one to reach it. Avery was right behind her. Jaelyn made it thirty seconds later. *I* was the rotten egg.

I swam out to the floating raft and pulled myself up onto it. "I've been practicing my dives. No more belly flops for me." I jumped off the float and dove into the water.

"Wow!" said Avery. "You barely made a splash. You *have* been practicing."

"Swimming every day helps," I said. "Sometimes I take a quick swim while you're taking your second riding lesson. It's just been so hot, it's the only thing that cools me off."

For the next fifteen minutes, we had a contest to see who the best diver was.

"Avery's the best," said Esha. "The best belly flopper, that is."

Avery stuck out her tongue at Esha and tried to dunk her.

"Good try," said Esha. Then she pushed Avery under the water. "But not good enough."

When Avery came to the surface, she let out a stream of water into the air.

"Hey," she said, "did you guys hear that Aunt Jane is taking us on a new trail this week? We get to ride the horses through a stream *and* a pond. The pond isn't very deep. She says it's perfect for the horses. They're going to love it."

"I wish I could go and watch," I said. "Sounds like fun."

"You sure you don't want to ride with us, Bree?" said Jaelyn. "I miss you out on the trails."

"Me too," said Avery. "We all do. Right, Esha?"

Esha shrugged. "Maybe a little . . . okay, a lot."

"Thanks. I miss spending the extra time together but I don't miss riding a horse. Honest. I'm glad you miss me and all but I have so much to do. I'll be teaching the Pony Girls in the morning, and I'm sure that's when you're going on the trail."

Avery nodded. "It's at nine thirty."

Esha looked surprised. "Do you have ESP or somethin'?"

"I wish!" I said. "Aunt Jane is rescheduling all trail rides and jumping lessons to the early morning to fit them in before it gets too hot."

"It's not that hot," said Esha. "When I visited my grandparents in India last summer . . . now that was hot! Hot with a capital *H*." She climbed out of the water and sat on the raft. She dangled her feet in the water.

"In fact, I *love* this weather. The hotter the better." She pointed to the shore. "You think I'm crazy? Look at that kid! He's wearing jeans and a long-sleeved shirt."

I cupped my hands over my eyes and spotted Brent drinking a bottle of water under some trees. He was talking to the little redheaded girl.

"That's Brent," I said. "He's the kid I was telling you about."

"Dr. Samuels's son?" asked Avery. "Why is he wearing long sleeves?"

I shrugged. "He says he doesn't want to get a sunburn."

Esha grabbed the sunscreen and swung her legs up onto the raft. "I'm goin' to bake in the sun. Maybe take a nap."

So while Esha soaked up the sun, we played water games with the girls from Cabin 3.

After an hour, I was tired of swimming. I got out of the lake, sat on a chair, and watched the girls play Marco Polo. I was just starting to think about my next class for the Pony Girls when Layla kicked off her flip-flops and sat down next to me.

"I heard you did a great job with the Pony Girls, Bree," said Layla. "Aunt Jane was proud of you."

"Thanks, Layla. It was so much fun. The Pony Girls are all so cute." Then I thought of the little redhead. "Except for the curly-haired girl. She was bratty."

Layla laughed. "That's Carly Jacobs. She has her sweet moments. She reminds me a little of Avery and a little of Esha, too." She dug her toes into the stony sand. "She has Avery's drive and Esha's bossy ways. Carly has her heart set on riding Sapphire. It's not going to happen. She's too young. And too bossy to be a good match for Sapphire."

Right in the middle of her third funny Carly story, Layla's walkie-talkie buzzed.

"Layla? Can you hear me? Come in, Layla."

I recognized Aunt Jane's voice.

"Go ahead, Aunt Jane," said Layla. "I hear you."

"I'm looking for Sapphire. Dr. Samuels wants to check her teeth. I don't see her in the stable," said Aunt Jane.

"Is she with Avery?" asked Layla.

I pointed to the water. "Avery's playing Marco Polo."

Layla frowned. "Scratch that. Avery is here in the lake. Did you check the log book? Was anyone scheduled to ride her?"

"No one signed up," said Aunt Jane. "Let me check with the rest of the gang. Stand by."

"That's so weird," said Layla. "Really weird."

"What's so weird about it?" I asked.

"That's the third or fourth time we've had trouble locating an animal in the past week," said Layla. "Isn't that odd?"

I thought about Golden Girl and Freckles.

"What do you mean *trouble* locating them?" I asked. "Are they running away?"

"No, nothing like that," said Layla. She leaned in and whispered. "Aunt Jane and I think someone's being careless. Or lazy. Maybe even both. Aunt Jane said that if she finds out who it is, she's going to fire them."

"Fire them?" I asked. "Would she really do that?"

"She wouldn't want to," said Layla. "But Storm Cliff Stables is her livelihood. She pays a lot of people to make sure the stables are run well. She takes pride in this place. If someone isn't doing his job, then she thinks that person doesn't belong here. She feels it's a reflection on her."

I decided to tell Layla about Golden Girl.

"She just vanished," I said as I snapped my fingers. "*Poof.* Just like that."

Layla tilted her head. "Well, Bree. I have to be honest. I don't think Golden Girl was missing at all. I have to agree with the rest of the Core Four. She was probably hiding behind the haystack. Or maybe she was out with Pip and Squeak in the pasture. She's a crazy chicken. You never know with her."

I wanted to tell Layla about Freckles. But if I did, I knew I'd get in trouble for being down at the barn after dark. Maybe even fired!

"Found Sapphire," said Aunt Jane's voice over the walkie-talkie. "All clear."

I gave Layla two thumbs up.

"Good," said Layla. "Where was she?"

"I'm not happy," said Aunt Jane. "She was tied to the hitching post behind the outdoor arena. She had plenty of water within reach but she shouldn't have been out there. Have you seen Bree? I asked her to cool down Sapphire after her morning ride with Avery. I really hope she wasn't the one who left Sapphire out all day."

Suddenly, I felt as if I couldn't breathe. I wanted to speak up but I couldn't find the words.

"Bree's with me, Aunt Jane," said Layla. "How about I send her to your office?"

"Tell her I'll see her in ten," said Aunt Jane, sounding grumpy.

I slid down in my chair and put my head in my hands.

"It wasn't me," I said. "I did cool Sapphire down. Then I put her inside her stall to rest. Honest."

Layla raised her left eyebrow. "I believe you, Bree. But it's not me you have to convince. It's Aunt Jane."

I suddenly had the feeling that my first day on the job was going to be my last.

I knocked on the screen door to Aunt Jane's office.

"Come in!" yelled Aunt Jane.

She smiled when she saw me. "Hey, Bree. Have a seat, will ya?" She narrowed her eyes. "You look scared, Bree. I'm not going to bite you. Promise."

I tried to smile but I couldn't. I squeezed my hands together and the words spilled out. "Aunt Jane, I didn't leave Sapphire outside in the sun. If it wasn't so hot, I probably would have let her graze. But in this heat? No way."

"Relax," said Aunt Jane. "I honestly never believed it was you."

I leaned forward in the chair. "You mean, you believe me? You're not going to fire me?"

She looked puzzled. "Why wouldn't I believe you? You've never given me any reason not to trust you. Right?" Then she laughed. "I wouldn't fire my best worker."

I thought about sneaking out to the barn to hang up the poster and look for Golden Girl. I bit my lip. I suddenly felt awful. If she knew, she'd fire me for sure.

"I just don't know who would be so careless," I managed to say. "Everyone here loves Sapphire. I can't think of anyone who would leave any horse out in this heat."

"I can't either," said Aunt Jane. "But not everyone cares quite as deeply about animals as you do, Bree. I think someone wasn't thinking. Being lazy, I suppose." She scribbled on a notepad. "But to be honest, I'm not sure Sapphire was out there all that long. When I saw her, I assumed she was there from the time you cooled her down. But when I brought her inside, she was fine. No signs of distress. Not overheated. It didn't look as if she'd even drank any of the water that was next to her."

She sighed. "Anyway, I totally trust you, Bree. So much so that I have something for you." She reached into her desk drawer and pulled out a box with ribbon tied around it. She pushed it across the desk. "Open it."

I pulled off the ribbon and slowly opened the box. Inside was a white shirt. "Does this say what I think it says?" I held it up. On the front, it had the Storm Cliff Stables logo. On the back, it said STAFF.

"When I saw you with the Pony Girls today, I just knew you were here to stay. I knew you'd be good with the girls. But I didn't know how *great* you'd be. Impressive!" She gave me a high five. "I don't think anyone here could have done a better job."

I hugged the shirt. "Thanks, Aunt Jane. I love it."

"I expect you to wear it each day when you're working with the Pony Girls. Being an official barn rat leader has certain perks, you know. A shirt is one of them. And although your mom said I can't officially pay you, I put twenty-five dollars into your account at the Green Canteen. Maybe you can treat the Core Four to some ice cream."

The Green Canteen is the camp store. It has

the *best* peanut butter horseshoe crunch ice cream treats.

I jumped up and gave Aunt Jane a hug. "I'll be one of the best campers you've ever had. I mean, one of the best workers you've ever had."

"You already are," said Aunt Jane.

When I got back to the cabin, the girls were changing out of their bathing suits. I told them the news.

"You're kiddin'," said Esha. "That's so cool. Isn't it, guys?"

"Way cool," said Jaelyn. "Too bad she can't pay you for real."

"I think getting paid at the store *is* real, Jaelyn," said Avery. "Don't you think, Bree?"

"Oh, I don't care about the money," I said. "I'm not even old enough to get a real job."

Avery put her hands on her hips. "But you do have a real job. You practically run the stable, Bree."

"Ha! I like to pretend I do, but I really just clean the stalls and . . ."

Esha interrupted. "Give *me* the money! I could buy six bottles of nail polish with that twenty-five dollars."

"Don't get any crazy ideas," I said. "But if you stop being so bossy, maybe I'll treat you to ice cream tomorrow."

"Deal," said Esha. "My lips are zipped."

Then I filled them in on Sapphire. "So she was missing too. At least for a few minutes. No one could find her."

Out of the corner of my eye, I saw Jaelyn smirk at Esha and Avery.

"What's wrong?" I asked Jaelyn. "Are you laughing at me?"

"I'm not laughing," said Jaelyn. She lowered her eyes. "It's just that . . ."

I felt my face getting redder by the second. "What?" I asked.

"You seem kind of obsessed with animals disappearing lately," said Jaelyn. "Sapphire wasn't really lost. It was just a mix-up."

"But Layla mentioned that three or four other animals have gone missing over the last two weeks, too," I said. "Do you think she's making it up?"

I suddenly didn't feel like treating any of them to ice cream.

"Let's just drop it," said Avery. She held up her brush. "Why don't we braid each other's hair for the campfire tonight?"

"Can't," said Esha. "I promised the girls next door I'd hang out for a while. But I'll see you at the campfire."

So instead of feeling good about my shirt, I ended up feeling mad. But I didn't want to cause any problems so I just braided Jaelyn's hair instead.

We were the last ones at the campfire. Again.

I spotted Dr. Samuels and Brent by the fire, so I went over to say hi. Brent was scratching his arms like crazy.

"Itchy arms?" I asked.

"I'm fine," he said. "I just got a little sunburned today."

"But you were wearing long sleeves. Can the sun get through that shirt?" I reached for his arm. "Let me see."

He pulled his arm away. "I'm fine."

Carly ran up to us. She was eating a peanut butter horseshoe crunch ice cream treat. "Bree! Guess what! I just rode . . ."

Brent covered her mouth and spoke firmly. "No talking with your mouth full, Carly. That's gross. Got it?" He slowly took his hand off of her mouth.

She laughed. "Yep. Got it." Then she held up her treat. "As long as I get more of these, I get it!" Then once she spotted the marshmallows on the picnic table, she ran off.

"Odd kid," said Brent as he followed her to the table and popped a marshmallow into his own mouth.

After talking to the rest of the Pony Girls, I hung out with the girls from Cabin 3 while we toasted marshmallows and sang camp songs. I was having a great time until I overheard Esha by the water station.

"Has anyone seen the ant that was just on the log?" asked Esha. "He's missin'!"

Avery and Jaelyn laughed.

"And the caterpillar that was on our cabin door today," said Avery. "Where did it go?" She pretended to bite her nails. "Oh no! She's missing!"

That made Esha laugh so hard she snorted.

They were making fun of me!

I stormed up to them. "Go ahead. Laugh all you want. See if I care."

"Oh, Bree," said Esha. "Lighten up. We're just jokin' around."

Avery nodded. "Sorry, Bree. I guess it wasn't very nice of us."

"You *guess* it wasn't very nice? *Guess?*" I had to blink my eyes really fast or else I would have cried. "Whatever," I said as I walked away from them.

When the campfire was over, everyone headed up the path.

Everyone but me. I veered off to the right and headed straight to the stables. I could see that a light was still on and I knew that there was usually somebody in there until midnight.

I walked inside and looked around. Queenie was in the first stall.

"Hey, Queenie." I grabbed a brush, put on my helmet, and ran it over her back. Then I decided to braid her tail as I told her my problems. After I finished, I looked at the clock. I had ten minutes until bunk check.

That gave me enough time to go say hi to the

other horses. I walked down the center aisle and stopped to say hello to each one.

It was peaceful this time of night. No tack to worry about. No getting sprayed by the hoses. No responsibilities.

But the peaceful feeling didn't last very long.

I heard a creaking sound at the opposite end of the stable. When I looked down the aisle, I saw the door close gently. Was someone spying on me?

I got a tingly feeling down my spine.

Something was wrong. I could feel it.

I quickly walked up and down the stalls and counted the horses.

That's when I knew.

One of the horses was missing.

But which one?

It only took me a minute to realize that it was Sapphire.

Don't jump to conclusions, I thought. *She has to be here somewhere.*

I walked into the indoor arena. I didn't hear anything. And after my eyes adjusted to the dark, I didn't see anything either. So I headed to the outdoor arena and poked around. There wasn't any sign of Sapphire, so I went back into the barn. After five more minutes of looking in each stall again, I knew Sapphire was gone.

Just like Golden Girl.

Just like Freckles.

I stood inside her stall. Her door had been

closed, so I knew she couldn't have wandered out by herself. Avery was going to be upset. Then I thought about the campfire. Maybe I was being a little dramatic. Maybe I did overreact. Just because Sapphire wasn't here didn't mean she was missing, did it?

I walked back out to the center aisle.

"What are you doing here?" It was Aunt Jane. She was holding a book in one hand and a radio in the other. "It's past curfew. Did Layla do bunk check yet?"

"I don't know," I said. I glanced at the clock on the wall. "She usually does it now."

Aunt Jane bit her lip. "Well get going, Bree. Unless you want to tell me what you're doing in here so late?"

My heart pounded. "I came to get away from the girls for just a few minutes. They were sort of teasing me at the campfire. I needed a break so I came to say good night to the horses. I was going to go straight back to my cabin but that's when I noticed one of the horses isn't here."

Aunt Jane looked alarmed. "A horse is missing? Who?"

"Sapphire. I don't see her anywhere," I said. "I checked both arenas. She wasn't there."

Aunt Jane rushed over to Sapphire's stall. "The door was left open. Careless, careless, careless," she muttered. "She's probably out wandering around. Maybe she's visiting the barn."

I shook my head. "Her door was closed. I opened it a minute ago, but it was closed when I got here. So she couldn't have left by herself."

Aunt Jane looked worried again. She spoke into her walkie-talkie and within a few minutes, Layla rushed through the door.

"She's not at the barn," said Layla. "And no one spotted her at the lake or the Pavilion."

She looked surprised to see me with Aunt Jane. "Should I double-check the arenas?"

Aunt Jane scratched her head. "Already did. Triple-checked them, actually."

"Where could Sapphire be?" I asked. "First she was left outside today, and now this?"

"It could be a coincidence," said Layla. "Or . . ." She looked at Aunt Jane.

"Don't even say it, Layla," said Aunt Jane. "I refuse to even think about that possibility."

"What possibility?" I asked. "What's wrong?"

Aunt Jane plastered a fake smile on her face. "Oh, nothing, Bree. Nothing to worry yourself about. Go back to your cabin and turn in for the night. You have the Pony Girls first thing in the morning. It's been a long day. Get some rest." Then she added, "There's no need to tell the others. I'm sure Sapphire will be back here soon enough."

I started to tell them I wasn't tired and that I wanted to help look for Sapphire, but Aunt Jane refused to listen. She pointed to the door. "Out." Then she smiled. "Sweet dreams."

But how could I have sweet dreams when I knew Sapphire wasn't in her stall?

When I got back to the cabin, the girls were painting their toenails.

"Where were you?" asked Avery as she looked at the clock on the desk. "You're lucky Layla hasn't been here for bunk check yet. She's late."

"Want your toes painted?" asked Esha. "Or fingernails?"

"No thanks." I changed into my pajamas and sat on the floor with them. I wasn't sure if I should tell them about Sapphire. I didn't want to upset Avery. She'd freak out if she knew Sapphire wasn't in the barn right now.

"Were you trackin' down more missin' animals?" said Esha. She smirked.

Jaelyn and Avery shot her a look.

No one said a word for a minute. Finally, Jaelyn spoke up.

"I'm sorry, Bree. I was just joking around.

Honest. But it wasn't very nice of me. I feel awful that you got upset."

"So do I," said Avery. "It was just a dumb joke that wasn't even funny."

Esha agreed. Sort of. "It was a *little* funny at first. But then I felt bad." She lowered her head. "I know I goof around a lot. My mom says I have to learn when to 'turn it off.'"

I felt a lot better until I thought about Sapphire.

"I don't know if I should tell you guys this," I said. My heart started to beat faster. "But if it were my horse, I'd want to know."

Esha slouched over. "Don't tell me another horse has gone missin'." Then she added, "For five whole minutes . . ."

"Well . . . would you want to know if a horse were missing from the stables? The horse you loved and rode every day?" I asked.

Avery and Jaelyn nodded.

"Yeah," said Avery. "I guess so."

So I told them about Sapphire.

"And then Aunt Jane told me to get some sleep. She said she was sure Sapphire would be in her stall in the morning."

Avery didn't look upset. Jaelyn yawned. Esha got up to get more nail polish.

"Isn't anyone worried about Sapphire?" I asked. I turned to Avery. "What about you?"

Avery took a deep breath. "Bree, I think maybe you're . . ."

"What," I asked.

"Fibbin'," said Esha.

I stood up. "Why would I lie?"

"Calm down, Bree," said Avery. "I didn't say you were lying."

I studied Avery's face. "But you were thinking it, weren't you?"

When she didn't answer, I knew it was true. I got up and threw my sweatshirt on over my pajamas. "I'll prove it to you. Let's go down to the stable. I bet Layla and Aunt Jane are still there."

I didn't have to convince them. Three minutes later, we were crouching under an open window at the stable. We could hear Layla and Aunt Jane talking.

"Do you think that's what happened?" asked Layla. "What are the chances?"

"Considering it happened just two towns away a few months ago," said Aunt Jane, "I think it could be a strong possibility."

"What are they talking about?" whispered Jaelyn.

"Sapphire," I said. "I think."

Avery shook her head. "They haven't mentioned any horse."

I motioned for her to keep her voice down.

"Should we call the police?" asked Layla.

Esha's eyes grew as big as saucers. "The police?" she mouthed to the rest of us.

"Too early to be calling anyone," said Aunt Jane. "But if Sapphire isn't found by daybreak, I'll ride out to High Point and search for her myself."

Avery gasped. "It's true! Sapphire's missing!"

"I'm sure she'll turn up," said Layla. "Don't you think?" Then we heard her say, "It doesn't make sense. There are younger horses. Stronger horses."

"What does she mean by that?" asked Avery.

I shrugged and moved my ear closer to the window.

"Layla," said Aunt Jane, "I have a terrible feeling about this. What if those men who stole the horses from the stables in Mount Holly came here and took her? I hate to say it, but I think they might have taken Sapphire."

My mouth dropped open.

"What did they say?" Avery asked as she tugged on my sweatshirt.

I took a deep breath and chewed on my bottom lip.

"Well?" said Avery. "Tell me."

I took a deep breath and blurted out the terrible news. "They said Sapphire has been horsenapped!"

"Horsenapped?" screamed Avery. She jumped up and burst through the stable doors. She ran toward Sapphire's stall. "Are you sure?"

Aunt Jane grabbed her arms. "Avery! What are you doing here? We don't know anything for sure. I was just commenting on some news I had heard around town over the last few months."

"Calm down. The horses are getting agitated," said Layla. She pointed toward Queenie, who had thrown back her ears and flared her nostrils.

I reached into my pocket and pulled out a peppermint for Queenie to calm her down.

"Are you sure she's missing?" asked Avery again. She looked out the stable window, frowning. "Where could she be?"

Aunt Jane shrugged. "We're going to find her. But there's really nothing you can do tonight. Get some rest. You have dressage and jumping tomorrow. And Bree, the Pony Girls are ready to learn some more from their favorite barn rat."

Avery folded her arms over her chest. "How can I even think about jumping tomorrow?" Then she started to cry. "Sapphire and I are a team. We jump *together*." She glanced at the empty stall. "Please let me go with you to High Point to look for her."

Aunt Jane held up her hand. "Avery, listen to me. A lot can change in a few hours. By the time you wake up, Sapphire could be back and ready to jump. But no matter what tomorrow morning brings, it's business as usual. Breakfast, riding, classes for the Pony Girls. Got it?"

"Got it," whispered Esha, Jaelyn, and I.

Avery didn't say a word.

As Layla started to talk, Aunt Jane pulled me aside.

"I know you were probably thinking you needed to tell Avery, Bree. But this just adds more stress to the situation. Please get Avery out of this stable. She's upsetting the horses. Bring her back to your cabin. Make sure she gets some sleep and is at breakfast by eight o'clock tomorrow. I don't want this to spread throughout camp and have everyone worrying about Sapphire." She sighed. "I'm not going to sugarcoat it, Bree. Sapphire *is* missing and I'm terribly worried."

Twenty minutes later, the Core Four were back in Cabin 4.

"I believe you now," said Avery. She blew her nose. "Sorry I didn't believe you before."

Esha handed Avery another tissue. "I bet Sapphire got bored and went explorin'. That's all."

Jaelyn nodded. "I think so, too."

Me? I wasn't so sure. "Does anyone here think there's a connection between the barn animals that went missing and Sapphire?"

Avery started to cry again.

Jaelyn shrugged. "We're not 100 percent positive that Freckles and Golden Girl were really lost."

"But remember what I told you about Layla? She said a few animals got 'lost' recently. And then when they couldn't find Sapphire today . . ." Then I had an idea. "Why don't we try to think of who the last person was to see Sapphire. Maybe that could help us."

Avery blew her nose again. "I rode her this morning. I was done riding at eleven o'clock. It was too hot this afternoon so I went to the lake instead of riding her again."

"I cooled her down and put her back into her stall at twelve o'clock," I said. "Then I had lunch with you guys."

Esha clapped her hands together. "I was with Sapphire at 6:10."

Everyone looked surprised.

"That's when I left the stable to meet everyone here before dinner. I remember looking at the clock when I left her."

"Why were you in the barn with Sapphire?" I asked.

"Well," she said. "It was goin' to be a surprise. That's why I told you I was goin' to Cabin 3. I didn't. I snuck over to the stable. I wanted to use Twinkle Toes Hoof Glitter on Queenie's hooves." She pointed to a small bottle on the desk.

"So I went to the stable to put it on her. That's when I saw that boy." She tapped her finger on her chin a few times. "What's his name?"

"Boy?" I asked. "Do you mean Brent? Dr. Samuels's son?"

Esha nodded. "He was in the stable. He had some tools with him. He asked me if I knew which stall Sapphire was in. He said he had to repair a plank inside. So I showed him. He knew a lot about Sapphire, like that Anna had learned to ride on her. He said that would make a great story. He kept askin' me all sorts of questions about ridin' a horse and how to feed them bits of apples and carrots. So I showed him how to do it."

Esha laughed. "He was afraid at first and dropped the carrot. Then he saw my Twinkle Toes Hoof Glitter in my hand and asked me what it was for. I told him I was going to use it on Queenie, so I showed him how it looked . . . on Sapphire."

Avery's eyes lit up. "Aw . . . I bet she looks so cute."

Esha agreed. "She does! If Sapphire comes back, you're going to love how it looks. It's a brand-new color. Her hooves are sparkly purple."

Avery's lip quivered. "*If* Sapphire comes back?"

Jaelyn spoke up. "*When* Sapphire comes back."

"So then what happened?" I asked. "It sounds like Brent was the last person to see Sapphire?"

"Nope," said Esha. "It was me. Brent left before I did. I still had to paint Queenie's hooves and then I came back here."

Esha yawned and stretched her arms out. "Oh! I did see one more person before I left the barn."

"Who?" I asked.

"It was a barn *brat*, Bree. That little redheaded girl."

"Carly Jacobs," I said. "What was she doing in the stable?"

"She wasn't exactly *in* the stable. She was at the door with Layla. She was beggin' Layla to let her ride Sapphire. But Layla just kept sayin' that Sapphire was too big for her. She was mad. She was so mad that she stomped her foot and then huffed and puffed her cheeks before runnin' away from the stable. Layla had to chase after her."

"So you were the last person to see Sapphire," I said. "That we know of. It was only an hour before the campfire. And then a few hours later, she was ..."

"Gone," said Avery.

Jaelyn hugged Avery. "I have an idea. Why don't you tell us some stories about Sapphire? It will make you feel better."

So while I tried to figure out who could have taken Sapphire, Avery told us stories about her until she fell asleep.

Since I couldn't sleep, I sat at the desk reading Avery's *Horse & Rider* magazines. That's when I noticed something interesting about the bottle of Twinkle Toes Hoof Glitter.

Something very, very interesting.

It wasn't Twinkle Toes Hoof Glitter at all.

It was a bottle of lotion.

Ivy-Off!

As soon as Avery got up in the morning, she wanted to find Aunt Jane.

"There's no news yet," I told her.

Avery rubbed her eyes. "How do you know?"

"I've been up for a long time. I've already done my chores at the barn. I saw Aunt Jane and Layla leaving. She said to tell you not to worry and that she hopes you ride Duke today. He needs to be exercised, and she won't be here to ride him herself."

She shook her head. "No way. I can't ride another horse right now. How could I concentrate? It wouldn't be fair to Duke."

"You can watch me jump," said Esha.

"No thanks," said Avery. "I think I'm just

going to hang around the stables today. Maybe I can help tack up some horses and muck the stalls with you, Bree."

"That's a great idea," I said. "I can use the help. But first I have to teach the Pony Girls. Want to come?"

"No thanks." She looked at Jaelyn. "Want to go for a walk? Maybe we'll see Sapphire."

Jaelyn often went on the marked hiking trail around the arenas in the morning. It was only a mile long but full of wildlife this time of day.

"Let's go," said Jaelyn. "Sapphire *could* be there."

"Me too," said Esha. "Then I want to go to the Green Canteen to get more Twinkle Toes Hoof Glitter."

The glitter! I went to the desk and picked up the bottle. "This isn't Twinkle Toes Hoof Glitter, Esha."

Esha came over to see it. She scratched her

head. "I must have left it in the stable and picked up this bottle by mistake."

"It's the same size bottle as the glitter," said Jaelyn. "What is it?"

"Ivy-Off," I said. "It helps stop the itching you get from poison ivy."

Esha dropped the bottle. "Poison ivy? I don't want to get that! The itchin' would drive me crazy."

"But what was this doing by the stalls?" I asked.

Esha shrugged.

I shoved it in my pocket. "Maybe it's Layla's or Aunt Jane's. I'll give it back to them when I see them."

I headed to the barn and saw Dr. Samuels.

"Did you hear the news?" I asked. "Someone took Sapphire. She's missing."

"I heard," said Dr. Samuels. "I saw Layla this morning. She and Aunt Jane were hopeful that

Sapphire just felt like exploring. Let's cross our fingers that they find her at High Point."

But when they returned from High Point during lunch, Aunt Jane and Layla had bad news.

"No signs of Sapphire," said Aunt Jane.

"We searched the entire area," said Layla. "Nothing."

Avery pushed her plate away.

"Don't give up hope," said Aunt Jane. "I'm certainly not going to."

I could tell Aunt Jane was upset, but I knew she had to pretend that she was fine.

"So how were the Pony Girls today, Bree?" she asked.

"They are so cute!" I said. "Today I taught them about the cows. We had class inside the barn and they got to milk Daisy. Did you know that none of the girls had ever milked a cow before?"

"None?" said Aunt Jane. "Really?"

"I was surprised, too," I said. "And guess what Carly wanted to do to Daisy?"

"Ride her?" said Layla.

Everyone laughed. Even Avery.

"She wanted to file her teeth!" I said. "She was mad when Daisy refused to open her mouth."

Layla put her hands up in the air. "Carly is a handful, isn't she?"

Aunt Jane got up. "Girls, my advice to all of you is to go swimming now. Take your minds off of things for a while, okay?"

"Don't feel much like swimming," said Avery. "If it's okay with you, I'm going to hang out in the stable."

"That's fine," said Aunt Jane.

"I'll go with you," said Esha.

"Me too," said Jaelyn.

"Me three," I said. "But I have to do something first. I'll meet you there in a few minutes."

So as they headed for the stables, I went in

the opposite direction to the Green Canteen. I had twenty-five dollars from Aunt Jane to spend and thought that some ice cream might cheer up Avery.

When I walked inside, I could hear someone laughing. It was Mrs. Matthews, who ran the store.

Without looking up from her computer screen, she asked, "May I help you?"

"I'm going to buy some ice cream," I said.

She laughed again as she pulled the screen closer to her.

I stood in front of the ice cream case and reached for four peanut butter horseshoe crunches.

"I'll take these, please."

Mrs. Matthews ignored me and went right on smiling and laughing.

"I'm ready," I said as I cleared my throat. "I'll take these, please."

"One minute, dear," she said. "This is almost over."

Finally, she came over to the counter. "That

kid has a bright future. Funny as can be. So charming, too."

"Were you watching a movie?" I asked.

"Oh, no! I was watching Dr. Samuels's son on the computer. He has his own website."

"Brent?" I said.

She nodded. "Do you know him? Such a funny boy. Charming."

"I know him. Not sure I think he's funny. At least not around me," I said.

"Impossible," she said. "Have you seen any of his shows?"

"Shows?" I asked.

She turned the screen around so I could see it. "He makes up cute little news reports. He calls them *Around Town with Brent Samuels*. He adds music and sound effects. He has such a wonderful sense of humor."

She pressed a button and Brent's face popped up. He had on a suit and tie.

"Today, I'm going to interview the greatest escape artist of all time. Now, you're probably thinking this is going to be a story about Harry Houdini."

A picture of Houdini flashed up on the screen.

"But you'd be wrong. Today, I'm going to introduce you to a pig. Not just any pig! This pig is the most famous pig-and-escape-artist in the world: Freckles."

"Hey! That's Freckles," I said. "I help take care of him!"

Five minutes later, I agreed with Mrs. Matthews. "You're right. Brent is funny."

"Oh, that's not even one of his best clips," said Mrs. Matthews. "Look here, he has dozens of them. Want to see another?"

I sat down and felt something wet on the side of my pants. "Oh no," I said as I pulled out the bottle of Ivy-Off. "This exploded in my pocket." I set the bottle down on the desk.

But Mrs. Matthews wasn't paying any

attention to me. She was too busy reading down the list of available interviews.

"He has stories about Aunt Jane, Golden Girl, Pip, Sapphire..."

"Sapphire?" I asked. "Can we watch it?"

That's when Mrs. Matthews noticed the bottle. "Oh my. Brent must have left this here. Poor boy has such a bad case of poison ivy. Three weeks now! I told him to stay away from it but he said he can't. It's all part of his job. Such a shame he has to cover it up in this heat."

I thought of the day I met Brent. *Didn't he say he wore long sleeves because he didn't want to get a sunburn?*

"Anyway," said Mrs. Matthews, "if you want to watch his show about Sapphire, we can."

She clicked on a link and the music started to play.

This time, Brent had added footage of Anna Wainwright in the Olympics. He even interviewed Aunt Jane and then ended it with a deep voice that made me laugh. *And to think that Anna's journey all started with a chestnut Thoroughbred mare named Sapphire at Storm Cliff Stables.*

He had the camera freeze on a close-up of Sapphire. Then, in slow motion, the camera moved back so you could see a whole shot of Sapphire.

I leaned in to take a closer look.

And that's when I knew that Brent Samuels wasn't just a liar. He was a horse thief, too!

Chapter 10
Nabbed!

I put the peanut butter horseshoe crunches back into the freezer. "Gotta go, Mrs. Matthews. I'll come back later for the ice cream."

"I can't promise that they will be here. That little redhead . . . what's her name?"

"Carly?" I asked.

"That's it!" said Mrs. Matthews. "Brent came in last night and early today saying he had to buy her some ice cream so she'd keep quiet."

Mrs. Matthews put a hand to her forehead. "My, that child has the gift of gab, doesn't she? I'm sure she's been talking Brent's ear off. In fact, she's been talking my ear off. She was just in here telling me all about her first ride on Sapphire last night."

"Last night?" I sucked in my breath. I thought about Brent covering Carly's mouth at the campfire.

Everything made sense now.

I stormed out of the Green Canteen and headed toward the barn. But I didn't go into the barn when I got there. Instead, I walked behind the barn and over to the fence that Brent had been working on. I peered down the poison ivy path.

I looked around to make sure no one was watching. Then I took a deep breath and stepped onto the path.

The pathway didn't look any different than the dozens of other trails that started at Storm Cliff Stables. Except for the poison ivy! It was everywhere. I itched just looking at it. I didn't really want to get poison ivy but if I could get Sapphire back, it would be worth it.

I only had to walk about a quarter of a mile before I found her.

"Sapphire!" I gently rubbed her neck and offered her a peppermint. "Avery is sure going to be glad to see you! Aunt Jane, too."

I untied her from a tree and was about to head back to camp when I spotted Brent walking toward us.

"You're a liar," I said. "And a horse thief. And you bribe little kids to keep them quiet."

He shoved his hands in his pockets. He didn't say a word.

"Stealing, Brent? Really?" I said. "Bribing an eight-year-old to keep quiet? You could go to jail."

His mouth dropped open. "Jail? But I didn't steal any animals! I borrowed them."

"Did you take Freckles and Golden Girl this week, too?" I asked.

He nodded. "How did you know it was me?"

"I didn't until I went to the Green Canteen today. Mrs. Matthews showed me your videos," I said. "I would never have known if you hadn't filmed a story about Sapphire and posted it last night."

Brent looked surprised. "How did you know I made the tape last night?"

I pointed to Sapphire's hooves. "Esha used Twinkle Toes Hoof Glitter last night. When I watched the video, I saw her hooves in the last shot. Her *sparkly* hooves."

Brent groaned. "How did you know I bribed Carly?"

"Mrs. Matthews said you bought Carly ice cream to keep her quiet. I knew Carly wanted to ride Sapphire. She was upset last night when Layla said no. I'm guessing she came back into the barn before the campfire and saw you with Sapphire and . . ."

He held up his hand. "If you want to know the whole truth, I'll tell you."

I nodded and sat down on a boulder.

"A few minutes before the campfire started, I

took Sapphire out of her stall to bring her here to film her. I went through one of the trails that led to the gate so no one would see me. But Carly saw me. She was trying to get Pip's attention in the pasture and she spotted me at the gate.

"Carly told me I wasn't allowed to go through the gate. I knew she'd tell on me and I had to keep her quiet. She said she wanted a ride on Sapphire. I didn't think it was a big deal.

"After she rode, she wouldn't go to the campfire unless I bought her ice cream. So, I bought some and then made sure she got to the campfire. Good thing, too, 'cause Layla was searching all over for her.

"I was going to head straight back here once the campfire started, film Sapphire, and put her back in her stall before the campfire ended but my dad saw me. I had to stay. That was a good thing actually because Carly was about to blab my secret to you. I covered her mouth and made a joke out of her talking so much." He paused for a moment. "So after it was over, I came back and filmed my clip under the lights."

He pointed toward two huge spotlights that were connected to an orange extension cord.

"But when I went to bring Sapphire back to the stable, I saw you there. I thought Aunt Jane was with you. And if she knew I had taken . . . I mean, *borrowed* a horse without permission, I'd get fired. I was scared. So I brought her back here until I was sure I could slip her back into the stable."

"Carly isn't allowed to ride Sapphire," I said. "She could have gotten hurt."

"I walked her real slow around the barn once. That was it." Then he groaned. "My dad is going to flip out when you tell him." Then he got angry. "It's all your fault, you know."

"My fault?" I said. "How is this *my* fault? I

didn't do anything wrong. You're the one who stole the animals."

"I was planning on bringing Sapphire back right away. Honest. But you are always in the barn or in the stable. And I didn't steal them. I told you I *borrowed* them. Borrowed them to make my videos. You know how my dad feels about me going to film school. He's not happy about it. In fact, he says that if I want to go to film school in New York City, I'll have to pay for it myself."

I was confused. "What does this have to do with Sapphire?"

"Everything! When I found out that Anna Wainwright learned how to jump with Sapphire, I knew it would make a great story. So I went into the barn before dinner last night."

"But Esha was there," I said.

He nodded. "I just needed to film her for a few minutes before the deadline today."

"What deadline?" I asked.

"I applied for a scholarship. If I win, I'll get free tuition and then my dad will have to let me go to the school. But to apply, I had to make three videos and submit them with my application. I had two that I knew were really good, but I needed another story. One with a different angle. I thought of Anna, her gold medals, and Sapphire."

Sapphire snorted.

"Why didn't you just ask for permission?" I said.

"Aunt Jane would have told my father. And if he knew I had been making videos right here for the last year, he'd really be mad."

"The last *year*?" I asked.

"I'm serious about it, Bree. My stories are good. I think I have a shot at winning that scholarship." He scratched his arm. "I never had a reaction to poison ivy before so I thought this was the perfect place to film. No one is ever here. It's private and not too far from the animals."

I thought of Freckles. "Freckles is so wiggly! How did you get him here?"

Brent laughed. "I put a leash on him and walked him here. He loved it! When I took, I mean *borrowed*, Freckles, I didn't know you were inside the barn with your friends. When I got Freckles out the gate, I saw your flashlight and I took off running."

"I *knew* there was someone out there that night!" I said. "I just knew it."

"And I made sure there was some food on the path for him to eat," said Brent. "I knew he'd keep moving along if he had food to eat every few feet."

The thought of Freckles on a leash made me laugh. "Is that why you threw apples and carrots over the fence? I saw you doing it but I didn't know why."

"Now you know," he said. He scratched his arm again. I handed him the lotion.

"Where did you find it?" he asked. Then he smacked his forehead. "I left it in the stable, didn't I?"

I nodded. "I have another question. Did you bring Pip here?"

Brent lowered his head. "Yeah. I feel awful about it. I didn't realize he got a nail stuck in his hoof."

"Two of them," I said. "Your dad and I had no idea where the nails came from. At least I know now." I looked around to see if I could see any nails on the ground. "That was really careless of you."

"Are you going to tell Aunt Jane?" said Brent.

"What do you think?" I asked.

He ran his hand along Sapphire's back. "Nope. You're going to make *me* tell her, aren't you?"

"Yep," I said.

I led Sapphire back to the stable and then Brent and I went to Aunt Jane's office.

After Brent told her everything, she leaned back in her chair and didn't say anything for a long time.

Finally, she spoke in a low voice. "I'm disappointed, Brent. Very disappointed." She rubbed her forehead. "I've known you since you were six years old. Did you really feel like you couldn't talk to me about this?"

Brent sighed. "You're good friends with my dad. I thought you'd be on his side."

Aunt Jane sighed. "I'm not on *anyone's* side. When you interviewed me, I had no idea you uploaded the video and were submitting it as part of your college application. I could have helped you. Instead, you hurt me. And Avery. And Bree here. And Layla . . . I could go on and on."

Brent's eyes filled with tears. I had to look away from him.

"I didn't know everything would get so messed up," said Brent. "And it is messed up. Big time."

"You know, Brent. I think you're a smart kid," said Aunt Jane. "A good kid."

Brent gave Aunt Jane a small smile.

"But even the nicest kids can mess up once in a while," said Aunt Jane. She pointed to me. "I'm sure Bree's messed up from time to time. I know I've messed up from time to time." She lifted a framed picture of Anna off her desk. "Heck, even Anna's goofed up."

Aunt Jane chewed on her bottom lip. "Okay, Brent. I think you've learned your lesson. I'm going to chalk this up to a learning opportunity. But no more borrowing anything without permission. Got it?"

"Got it," he said. He reached into his back pocket and took out a key. He placed it on her desk. "It's for the paint closet."

Aunt Jane stood. "Keep it. You're going to need

it. You have to repaint the barn this week."

Brent smiled. "I do? I'm not fired?" He did a fist pump.

"I wouldn't celebrate yet, Brent. You still need to talk to your father and explain everything to him. And talk to him about college. Tell him how serious you are about your goal. If the videos are as funny as Bree says they are, show him. He'll come around." Aunt Jane pointed to the door. "He's in the Pavilion doing some paperwork."

I got up to leave too.

"Not so fast, Bree. I wanted to thank you. You really saved the day. This could have had an unhappy ending." She pulled her clipboard off of a shelf. "What are you teaching the Pony Girls this week?"

"I could teach them about the goats," I said. "Or maybe the sheep. Or . . ." I smirked, "how about I teach them how to be the best animal detectives in the whole wide world?"